HOW TO BE A GOOD STUDENT AND A SUCCESSFUL PERSON

Goddy Obasi

OHIO . TEXAS . LONDON. TORONTO . LAGOS

How to be a good student and a successful person

Cover Design: Charles Fate (Notch Designs)

Published by:
Eleviv Publishing Group
Ohio | Texas | London | Toronto | Lagos
www.elevivpublishing.com
info@elevivpublishing.com
1-800-353-0635

ISBN: 978-1-952744-00-6

Printed in the United States of America

10 9 8 7 6 5 4 3 2

This book is dedicated to every man and woman, known
or unknown, who is earnestly impacting the principles of
this book to the younger generation. I salute them all

Table of Contents

Introduction

I have always wanted to empower more than one student at a time, remind them that they can dream big, set goals, plan strategically, and work towards achieving their goals. After all, failure and success start from the mind.

When we learn, we need to teach others what we learned. Otherwise, those experiences become meaningless. My goal for writing this book is to share my experiences as a student, and hopefully, many students will learn from my mistakes. Information is indeed power, but applied information is more powerful. This book will help students avoid the paths that could lead to poverty of the mind, poverty, and regrets in the future. This book is not a "trial and error" kind of book, but an eye-opener; call it a Guide if you may. It will also help students understand what it means to become educated because education is more than getting a degree or certificate.

The reality is that many teenagers and young adults do not think about their futures. They live in the *'here and now.'* Many millennials also believe that being in school is a favor to their parent or guardian. If someone had shared their experiences with me to help guide me on the right path, I wouldn't have been lost. This book will show students how to discover themselves, build confidence, believe in themselves, be determined and focused on becoming a brilliant student, be successful against all odds, discover their purposes in life, and set goals to achieve them. I have experienced school life filled with failures and mistakes in some areas and others' success and achievements. The purpose of this book is to let you know and try to avoid the pitfalls. The principles work when you put them to practice. No matter the country you live in or your skin color or background, the results are the same. My goal is to share some of my life's lessons, so you can avoid the pitfalls I experienced. The principles work when you put them to practice; no matter the country you live in, your skin colour, or background, the results are the same.

Road to Success

"Life is like a box of chocolates; you never know what you are going to get." Some people were born with silver spoons in their mouths, while others, into poverty. However, being rich or poor is a thing of the mind. As a human being, you wish for a good life, especially when your life has not been on a bed of roses. For instance, some students want to have wealthy parents, supportive relatives, famous friends from affluent homes, or study abroad. As a student, you could be wishing you were smarter than your friends or classmates, improve your score in Mathematics or Economics, live in a fair and safe environment, or simply want to eat more than one meal a day.

Who doesn't like good things? Well, most people do. But the reality is those good things don't always come to you just because you are wishing for them or working hard to have them. Life is meant to be that way.

Ever heard, *"When life gives you lemons, make lemonade?"* When you are not one of the privileged ones, born with silver spoons in their mouths, you work extra hard to be your best, do your best, and live your best life.

Regardless of how almost perfect someone's life seems to be, nobody has it all because nobody is perfect, for perfection is an illusion, just like fear. Life is not easy in many parts of the world and more challenging in so many other aspects. Over the years, as a student, I had my share of struggles. I know how it feels to be hungry. I remember those sad days I'd go to school on an empty stomach and then get home and find the covered pots still empty. Fear is indeed an illusion, but it has a way of creeping in on you and instantly cripples you. My parents were either unable to pay my tuition or late in paying it; this caused me to lose focus when studying for an exam or test and even made me live in the fear that I might not be allowed to take tests or my final examinations.

In life, there are seasons, and each season has its time and reasons. Obstacles sometimes are meant to either delay us or reroute our directions to get us to our destined path. Experiences aren't supposed to break us; we can learn lessons from them; this is why I believe going through several experiences is going through life itself. The keywords here are 'go through.' Nothing in life is permanent. Therefore, what you are going through is seasonal, and you should not allow it to defeat you or take your joy away.

God's intentions for us as His children are good and not to harm or break us.

Did you know that seventy percent of famous and successful men and women were born and raised in abject poverty? Read that question again. People like Modi, the Prime Minister of India, went from being a tea seller to becoming a leader or Mike Adenuga, a taxi driver, and later, founded Global Com.

Sometimes, God uses hardship to humble our spirits or save our lives. When you allow your situation to misguide or break you into becoming a gang or cult member or choose to be a prostitute, you live in fear and not trusting God or your dreams. The hope of creating a better life for you and your family should humble you and help you stay focused.

How to be a good student and a successful person

I teach my students to be as authentic as possible. Being true to yourself is priceless. Also, being true to others is an added value. When you are trying to be like others, you will lose yourself in the process. How to become successful is to first know who you are or discover who you are. Knowing your strengths and weaknesses will help you understand yourself and become your authentic self.

Each time you draw strength from your weaknesses, you are discovering or rediscovering yourself. Tell yourself that no matter the obstacle that comes your way, it will be gone with the wind, just like every season.

When you make time for yourself and spend time with yourself, you will inadvertently learn how to be still, meditate, resist the urge to become your worst self, and you just might hear the voice of God speak to you. In doing so, you will find inner peace and joy while acquiring knowledge of who you are and meant to be to become the best version of yourself. Eventually, you will start focusing on what matters or should matter to you. You will start thinking like a responsible adult, though you are still somewhat a kid.

Ever heard of, *"Be wiser than other people if you can, but do not let them know?"* It's natural to want to be wiser than others. It's also natural to want to learn and be your best. The only way to grow is to be open to learning daily. But, you must practice, practice, and practice to be your best self. Reading how to be successful is a great way to acquire knowledge. But if you do not apply the information or the knowledge gained, the process and experience become meaningless and a waste of time.

It's essential to continually make positive affirmations that will uplift your spirit, energy and guide your steps. Each day, make a conscious effort to make a difference in your life.

Accept and Believe in Yourself

One of the biggest mistakes many students make is wishing to look like others. Even adults fantasize about being in someone else's shoes; after all, *"Grass is always greener on the other side."*

When you look in the mirror, who and what do you see? It is disheartening when young girls and boys in the mirror do not see themselves and wish they look like those beautiful and handsome students in their classes. Having low self-esteem is not appreciating one's inner and physical beauty. In many cases, physical beauty has its advantages, but your integrity is more attractive and valuable and appreciated by those who have integrity.

Believe it or not, there is something you have that the individual you wish to be like does not have. We are all unique. Specific traits make us who we are and shouldn't be. If or when we do not know those traits, how do we become the best versions of ourselves as intended by God?

Just remember that nobody has it all. Nobody!

Learn to stop complaining about what you don't have or wish to have, and start appreciating everything you have. There is more than one reason that you are you and look the way you look. God does not mold ugly. He made you beautiful and unique and His image. There is a purpose why He created you and filled you with all the great qualities that you have.

Your conception may have been unplanned; you may have been an unwanted child for one reason or another. You may have been born into a low-income family. Whatever your situation is or was, God knows all about you and knew you before you were born. Therefore, He also equipped you with all the necessary tools you need to be the best of you, grow, and succeed. So, stop wishing to be another person or be in their shoes.

I love and believe what Max Lucado said, *"You aren't an accident. You weren't mass-produced. You aren't an assembly-line product. You were deliberately planned, specifically gifted, and lovingly positioned on this earth by the Master Crafts-man."*

Therefore, accepting and believing in yourself is the first step to being successful. The reason is simple: If you do not accept yourself, you will start to dislike yourself, become lazy, start making up excuses for why you are unproductive, blame everyone and everything else for your failure & misery, and then end up living an unfulfilled life.

Psychologists have long said that if people do not accept who they were created to be, they develop an inferiority complex. When they have this mentality for a long time, they inadvertently self-hate.

Lack of self-love is the main reason many teenagers and young adults engage in reckless and shameless behaviors. For instance, a young girl filled with deep self-love, integrity, and high self-esteem would most likely, not engage in prostitution. With these positive traits, she will most likely resist certain temptations that may come her way.

A young boy filled with the same character traits as the girl would choose not to join a gang or secret cult. The anticipation of the shame when he gets caught would be enough to stop him from joining a gang.

THE STORY OF SAM

On February 15, 1980, an automobile accident happened along Benin-Lagos Expressway in Nigeria, leading to the fatality of 12 passengers. It was a head-on collision between a commercial bus and an 18-wheeler loaded with cows. There were dead cows and human bodies littered all over the Expressway, with blood running like a river.

Amongst the dead were Mr. and Mrs. Alex Mgbenesemeh. Their only son, Sam, survived but sustained bruises and a broken ankle. He was ten years old. After Sam was discharged from the hospital, his maternal uncle, who lived in Kano, came for him, and they went back to Kano.

Back in Kano, Sam's uncle's only means of survival was hawking bread on busy roadsides. He adopted Sam and trained him to help in his bread business. While his biological children never missed a day in school, Sam became a victim of child labour and didn't have the same opportunity to get an education, even though it was free education in the North.

By age 15, Sam looked twice his age from hardship, malnutrition, and severe depression. He had contemplated taking his life more than once.

One day, a well-dressed Muslim man saw him roaming the streets aimlessly and mistook him for an almajiri. He approached Sam and offered him lunch. The kind man started talking to Sam and felt his pain. He empowered Sam to consider thinking positively and give life a chance. He finally said to Sam, *"In this life, try not to depend on anybody, but on God, and then, believe in yourself."*

Sam told me that when the man completed the statement about depending on God, he stood up, left him where they both stood, and walked away. The strange Muslim man disappeared before Sam could open his mouth to say thank you. That was the turning point in Sam's life. For five years, Sam had depended solely on his uncle, who was inconsiderate of his future. Sam knew that his life was not going to be the same after that day. He was determined to become better, successful, and happy.

Many years later, Sam put himself through school, graduated with a second class upper in Business Administration from the University of Lagos, Nigeria, and eventually became a Lagos bank manager.

In one of my interviews with him, while preparing to write this book, I asked him to share his secrets to success and how he persevered. *"The secret is simple,"* he said. *"First, you should decide that you want to succeed, and second, take steps to lead you to success, and be determined to succeed. A determination is a fire, while the action is the fuel,"* he concluded.

Having shared Sam's success story, be determined to succeed because God has given you what you need to achieve success. Arthur Williams said, "The number one problem that keeps people from winning today is a lack of belief in themselves." There was an International Psychology Conference held in Europe, where renowned psychologists conducted research.

After months of research, these experts concluded that every child is a potential genius.

You are a potential genius. Start trusting and believing in yourself and your ideas. Accept who you are and the better version of yourself that you want to be. Believe that you can, work towards your goals, be determined, and you will succeed. All things are possible to those that believe.

YOUR MIND IS A POWERFUL TOOL

When Abdul Okpanachi was a bare-footed primary six pupil in Maranatha Primary School, Wukari in former Gongola State (now Adamawa), Nigeria, his teacher informed the class that there was going to be a quiz. Abdul went home and told his mother. His mother studied the material and gave him the answers to the test.

When the results came out, Abdul failed woefully. He only got two right answers out of 15 questions. His friend, who got 14 correct answers, told him that he studied for less than one hour for the test. But when Abdul told his friends that he had studied with his mother all through the night, they started laughing, mocking him, and called him *"otondo."* Ashamed, he found a quiet place and cried like someone had died.

That one experience made Abdul believe that he was not intelligent enough to be in school, thus, made him hate school. He allowed his friends' mockery and opinion of him to affect his mindset and decision. Abdul lost faith in himself and his fate.

The only way forward for Abdul was to detox all the negative comments in his head, start thinking positively, and seeing himself in a new light. He needed to be determined to be better and to succeed. He also needed to know that, *"He who has failed is he who thinks he has failed. He who will succeed is he who thinks he will succeed."*

The mind is a powerful tool. What we tell it stays in it. When we allow what others say to us to affect us, good or bad, they stay.

One of the world's best tennis players, Venus Williams, once said, *"You have to believe in yourself when no one else does. That's what makes you a winner."*

Believe in yourself, even when your friends or parents do not. Even when your classmates mock you or your teacher tells you that you will not succeed, believe in yourself. That, my friend, is the beginning of your success story. Start now to make complimentary use of your mind. Tell yourself that you are capable of succeeding. Rather than worrying about not having a sponsor to further your education, start thinking that somehow, somewhere, help will find you. God always makes a way when you trust Him.

Recent research about the brain indicates that the brain gets what it expects. Therefore, if your mind always expects disaster or always thinking that things will worsen, they always do. But if you always think optimistic about life and outcomes, things often turn out in your favor.

How does the brain attract what is in your mind to you? The process is called the 'Reticular Activating System.' This system involves the Elimination Method. The brain eliminates thoughts that aren't related to what you always think about. When it stops those thoughts, it allows you to concentrate on thoughts that are related to what you always think about. It would then begin to attract to you the things that you feed your mind. It will attract you to people and the material things that would help you achieve what you are thinking about or wishing for. Now you see why you should always think positively and eliminate failure from your mind?

TO ACHIEVE IS A DECISION

Remember that accepting yourself is the easiest road to success. Accepting who you are, means that you have decided to grow and achieve success. God predestines your success. Therefore, your true-self is linked to who you choose to become. Every architectural building starts from the foundation. The same applies to life. When you accept that you are a gift from God, therefore, destined to succeed, you are on the road to achievement. Realize who you are and achieve.

Jim Rohn is a self-made millionaire and speaker who guides young people on how to succeed in life. He has taught thousands of people who are growing in different areas of their careers and businesses. Rohn said, *"You must take personal responsibility. You cannot change the circumstances, the seasons, or the wind, but you can change yourself. That is something you have charge of."* I agree with Rohn and hope many of you will agree too and apply this wisdom in your lives.

Many years ago, I met a man named Samuel Adeyemi at a Speakers Conference; we were both Keynote Speakers; his likable personality instantly struck me. He was a self-confident man. After the conference was over, we officially met at the hotel. The first question I asked him was, *"How did you build self-confidence? What is the secret of your success?"*
"I will tell you a story. You see, I grew up in abject poverty at Ajegunle in Lagos. Life was tough. Back then, it was normal for many young men and women to be dealing with or on drugs, gambling, be a gang member, or go into prostitution or become a pimp. We did not understand the consequences of our actions. We believed that we were having the best times of our lives, he replied with a sad face and then smiled in between. *Until on that faithful Friday, my childhood friend, Ake, was found dead in the dumpster. He was stabbed to death, with his genitals chopped off. I will never forget the sight of his naked, lifeless body."* Yemi, as I fondly call him, continued.

As I listened to his story, my heart was breaking too. He told me that the night before Ake was murdered, they had had a smoke together. His brutal murder led him, Yemi, to think about changing his lifestyle and think about the rest of his life. He instantly denounced his gang membership and moved from Ajegunle to Isolo to live with his oldest brother. For the first time in his adult life, he started to think about his two younger sisters and widowed mother. Sometimes in life, it takes some tragic experience to be your wake-up call.

Yemi was determined to have a better life. So, he started to look for work. Luckily for him, he was employed part-time in a bakery. He knew he also needed to get an education. After work, he attended evening classes at a local school. He ended his tale by saying, *"During my reformation, I realized that the secret to success is self-discovery."*

I agree with Yemi's secret to success. Self-discovery can open doors that lead to success. Ajegunle remained Ajegunle. Some gang members remained as members because it was all they knew and open. The only thing that changed was Yemi's mindset. Today, he is a successful man and now teaches young men and women how to get motivated and succeed, discover their passions, and take control of their lives.

You do not need to wait to lose a loved one to wake up or put yourself in a situation that could cost you everything and possibly put your life in jeopardy. Discover yourself and who you are meant to be; don't let your friends or best friends control and mislead you. Stephen Arterburn and David Stoop wrote a fascinating book titled, *'Take Your Life Back.'* It teaches us how to stop letting the past and other people control us.
If you want to be a good student and become a successful person, you must decide to take your life back.

Practical Steps to Discover Yourself

Many students always ask, *"How do I discover myself? My friends always control and influence me. How do I take control of my mindset?"*
In answering these two relevant questions, you need to understand that the universe wants us to be aligned with its forces, all its positive energies. As humans, we sometimes, or most times, want to gravitate to others' energies nudging us to act like them, regardless if it's good or bad. Sometimes, it could merely be peer pressure.

The truth is that the universe sometimes puts us all in one basket so that we do things because friends, others in our social circle, school, community, friends, or classmates, are doing so. Thus, we are controlled by our environment.

Research has shown that youth delinquency is a result of environmental and peer pressure influences. So, how does one discover self and resist this environmental and peer pressure influence? How does a student overcome this powerful force that pulls us to do things we do not wish to do intentionally?

The answer is a simple old age method used by philosophers, *"Meditation."* Others say it's being alone with God. Many refer to it as having a quiet time, *"Me Time."* But, what's called is not the issue here. The bottom line is for you to put it into practice, and the result is impressive, a win-win. Start today. Do not wait another day to discover yourself and your purpose in life. Look for a quiet place to have absolute solace. It doesn't matter where you go, so long as it's safe and quiet. There are many great places to be alone and meditate.

In our world today, almost everybody is on the fast lane, always in a hurry. Not pacing yourself can cause tension that leads to unnecessary arguments and chaos. When you are stressed, you lose focus and possibly, self-control and perspective.

When you spend time alone, away from the noise, you will understand yourself better and build inner strength. It's never a waste of time when you have a me-time, and apply yourself by releasing all your negative energy. You invest in yourself when you spend time understanding your strengths and weaknesses. You are planting seeds in your life and filling yourself with inner power and strength. These will eventually help you make the right choices when your friends choose to go on the wrong path. You might even bother saving grace, just because you know better.

The core of who you are is your inner power, and it will always remind you who you are, value yourself more, and focus on your life goals. The big question now becomes, 'What would I be thinking about or meditating on when I'm alone?'

Well, you will be thinking about your future, starting from where you are to where you want to be. You might be thinking about God. You will remember your past—even your childhood. Simply meditate on every aspect of your life.

If your ambition is to become a medical doctor, imagine yourself in your white coat. Visualize it. Always hold on to that mental picture. Do not worry so much about how you are going to achieve it. Time for meditation or having quiet time is not time to be burdened, but to release your worries.

Warning! Bear in mind that the initial stage of this exercise may not come easy, and you just might get discouraged. Don't! Why would you be discouraged? Well, you are thinking about your future. That's something big and can be a bit scary. It's like having pre-wedding jitters. One student asked me, *"Why should I be thinking about my future when I have not had a meal all day? Another asked, "I cannot think on an empty stomach." Your mind could be you, 'You do not have a sponsor for your education, so you can't be thinking of becoming a medical doctor."*

Lots of such thoughts and questions could creep in on you as a begin-ner. It happens, and to so many others, it occurred to me. But, try not to listen to those voices. They are voices that want to stop you from progress-ing.

After the first few times, you will become comfortable and know how to filter thoughts that count. When you are persistent in self-control and self-discipline, dismissing those voices become a habit. It's like riding a bike for the first time. You fall. You get up. You get back on. Fall again. Get up, and ride again until you become a master in riding your bike. It's also right about meditation; determination is your key here; it is the key to learning any new skill.

Worry is an enemy of progress. If you wish to know how deadly worry is to goals and ambitions, go and look for Dale Carnegie's book, *'How to Stop Worrying and Start Living.'* The writing is brilliant and contains compel-ling messages. It will shock you with shreds of evidence that you are worrying yourself unnecessarily. Time of meditation and thinking about yourself and God is not the time for worry. It is time to submit to God and conquer yourself. It is time to beat peer pressure. It is time to conquer environmental influences. It is time to gain the momentum that would catapult you to be a good student and become a success in life.

Meditation is a habit that is worth acquiring for life. It would take you far ahead of your peers who do not make time to reflect on their lives and their future. Remember what Napoleon Hill said, *"If you do not conquer self, you will be conquered by self."* What does this mean? Simply, if you do not regain control of your mind, you will be controlled by the minds of others. Remember also the admonition of Lao Tzu, *"He who gains victory over other men is strong, but he who gains victory over himself is all-powerful."*
Become a role model for your peers. Become a role model in your neigh-borhood and for the youth. Philip Stanhope, 4th Earl of Chesterfield, once told his children, *"Be wiser than other people if you can, but do not tell them so."* Be wiser than your friends and classmates.

Never lose faith in yourself. Create new hope. Become motivated, inspired, and develop the desire to succeed. Don't wait for tomorrow to come, because tomorrow might never come. All we have is today. Choose from now to become successful by being a good student. Having the desire to change is vital. It is what will propel you to use this principle of meditation to discover yourself. Your parents will not do it for you; your teachers will not do it for you; your school mates and friends will not do it for you; the power is in your mind and hands. You need to choose to embark on the journey to get to your purpose in life, and the best way to learn how to swim is to jump into the swimming pool.

Knowledge is Power

The above statement is true. You need the knowledge to grow and succeed. If you want to succeed as a farmer, the more knowledge of farming you acquire, the more you apply what you learned to become a better and successful farmer. Education is a short cut to success.

Many adults who did not earn a certificate or degree have regrets. If you have a parent or relative who did not get an education, ask them how it makes them feel, especially when they had the opportunity but did not take it. Sometimes, other factors are not our obstacles. We are our biggest problems, our mentality, that is. Make use of your time when you are young to plan your life; your success or failure is in your hand. Do not misuse your time and be filled with regrets in your old age.

You may not realize the opportunity you have at your young age to succeed. You may not realize the chance you have until it's too late. The time to take action and a stand to become a better student is now. Challenge yourself. Use your weakness as your strength. Persevere, no matter the obstacle that may come your way.

Many young people make this common mistake; they do not envision their future. They live in the moments. This explains why most of them are easily swayed into joining bad gangs or secret cults. Many of them are murdered, or they destroy their future in the process.
But your case should be different. Have an ambition, set goals, and work towards achieving them. Praying and wishing will not work unless you apply knowledge and hard work.

Another common mistake many students make is thinking that going to school is doing their parent's favors. You are in school to better yourself and create a path for a brighter future. True that our parents are proud of us when we display academic excellence, and our teachers are happy when we behave well in school and focus on our studies. Therefore, it is no favor to your parents.

Other than being a lawyer and a Motivational Speaker, I am also a writer. You do not know my father. Everywhere I go, people that know me to shout out my name – Barrister Obasi! It feels good to be recognized. It gives one a sense of importance. It makes you feel worthy. It's a fact that teachers are the most underpaid workers globally. They teach us, train us, empower, inspire, and counsel us to become better men and women. Remember, when you ignore your teacher, you are cheating yourself out of gaining knowledge. Before you know it, time passes, and it's too late. Take your life seriously now that you are young to have a brighter future and share your knowledge. Stop looking for who you to blame for not studying and making good grades. Stop blaming lack of money or your parents for not supporting you enough, and stop blaming your English teacher for "being wicked."

Stop looking for who to blame and start looking for how to overcome the obstacles. No matter the problem, know that you have the power to rise and be determined to rise. It all begins and ends in your mind.
One wise man said to one of his students, and I agree, *"Your determination to succeed is the only one thing that would see you through in this life."*

Your success and happiness depend on what you know. So, seek knowledge and be empowered. Be on a quest to succeed as if your life depends on it. Remember, ignorance is the number one cause of death in Africa, as illiteracy is the leading cause of poverty.

Look around you and count how many adults who did not get an education struggle to make a living. They do menial jobs and get the lowest pay. They are the wheelbarrow pushers, groundnut sellers, welders, bricklayers, drivers, and cleaners. They live paycheck to paycheck. Would you like to be any of the above? The ball is in your court. Learn how to play and win.

Many students mainly focus on wearing the latest hairstyles and stylish uniforms to school. They want to be the "big" boys and girls. They want other students to respect them as those who know what's up.

There is nothing wrong with wearing the latest hairstyles and designer clothing. But there is everything wrong when you lose sight of what matters to secure your future. Be aware that many of those who are the *"big boy or girl"* in your school today most likely would end up dropping out. I remember some of the "big boys or girls" back in school. They were feared, respected, and imitated. But at the end of the day, they failed woefully. Leaving what is most important and focusing on what's not is the root of many students' failures. Make friends with those who take their studies seriously. No matter how their hairstyle or fashion sense, make friends with them, even as study partners. Do not destroy your future for any reason. Knowledge does not go out of fashion, just like your hairstyle or designer clothes.

Your destiny isn't tied to others. Do not let them choose you as friends. Be the one to choose your friends. Choose like mind friends. In doing so, you will begin to encourage one another. Iron sharpens iron. Birds of the same feather flock together. Ever heard this phrase, *"Show me your friends, and I will tell who you are?"*

Research shows that students who are not serious with their studies are always those who are most likely to lead others into cultism, prostitution, and gambling. Since they are not academically serious, they usually find other ventures to keep their minds busy, no matter who they hurt in the process. A person's mind cannot exist in a vacuum. Since they choose not to get busy with school and study, they get busy with unnecessary activities that will not enhance them.

You are the one who has decided to be a good student and grow into a successful adult. Why should you keep reckless friends with no ambition?

"Knowledge is power, but applied information is more powerful.". Avoid bad influences. They are destiny destroyers. Some of them have terrible upbringings. So, they come to school, looking for who to destroy and take down with them. Do not let them make you their victim. You are different from them. They can be different if they choose to. You are a child of destiny. Become ambitious to be the best of you, and achieve. Your success starts when you decide to succeed. It begins when you learn to say NO to harmful external factors. It forms the moment you discover or rediscover yourself.

If you do not have that inner power and self-control, your peers can and will easily deceive you into becoming the worst version of yourself. Start taking responsibility for your thoughts and actions. Be in charge of your life a hundred percent. Do not let your friends and mates negatively affect the way you think. What you think you do. Be wise! You are in school to acquire knowledge and not to make friends. You are not in school to be popular, neither are you there to win a beauty contest. You are in school to gain knowledge to become the successful person God created you to be.

No Dull Brain

"Every child is a potential genius!" Everyone has the power to be exceptional. These statements are factual. God wants a good life for each of us. The problem is that many of us do not use our common sense when need be. Sometimes, we are not the ones to be blamed. Most times, the students who fail a class test is not to be blamed. The fault lies with our teaching methods or lack of the needed emotional support from our parents. We do not always have people to encourage and root for us, but those that do not hesitate to condemn us. Many students experience verbal abuse from their parents. In the process, they lose their self-esteem and faith in themselves.

Words have the power to destroy or build. When you hear these negative statements from your parents, teachers, and friends, and you allow them to take roots in your minds, you will begin to believe that they are right. That's for sure! We live in a society where struggling to survive makes people quick to anger. And when they are quick to anger, they say what they are not supposed to say to their children. When a child does not understand you, most times, it means your approach is not effective. Change your approach. No two students are alike in understanding. Every child has a peculiar way God wired him to understand easily. Some learn fast when you show them love and compassion, and others when you shout at them. Some understand fast when scolded. Yet, some learn better when you show them love and compassion. This last group wants to know that you empathize with them and understand what they are going through. No student or child learns when you condemn and bully them. Condemning them makes his case worse; instead, teach and empower them.

While working on this book, I read an interesting story about a student who was doing poorly in class. He came from an impoverished background. His teacher tried her best, but the boy failed. The teacher was either doing something wrong, or the boy has underlying issues that hindered him from assimilating what was being taught. There's always a reason why some things happen. His teacher wrote a letter to his parents, and it read as:

Dear Mr. and Mrs. X,

I regret to inform you that your son failed again. I have done my best to help him. Please save your money; your son cannot be helped; he is dull and unintelligent. Kindly find some craft for him to learn, rather than sending him to us. Our school or any other school cannot help him. Thank you.

Sincerely,
Ms. Gloria

When the boy's mother read the letter, she was shocked. But in order not to dampen her son's spirit, she said to him: *"Your teacher said you just need more encouragement. She also said you are bright and intelligent, but they do not have the skill to bring out the intelligence inside you, and to find another school with teachers who can."*

That boy went to another school, became more self-confident, carried that image in mind that he wanted to be a success, and he was. One day, after his mother had passed away, he was going through some documents and saw that letter. When he read it, he understood what his mother did on that day. All he could do was cry. They were tears of joy. He had an amazing, loving mother. She chose to motivate her son when his teacher condemned him.

Can you imagine if his mom had behaved like his teacher? He would have been demoralized for sure and lose faith in himself. When someone condemns you, it is their loss. You are a potential genius. You have every-thing deposited in you for success.

How to Study and Understand

Everybody does not have the same amount of intelligence. There are low, medium, and high IQs - Intelligence Quotients. No matter your IQ level, the bottom line is that you are intelligent.

In the last chapter, I stated that our education system and our teachers in Nigeria are to be blamed when students fail. The reason is that teachers use the same methods to teach all students regardless of the subjects. Every student's level of reasoning and understanding differs. There are three types of learners; fast learners, slow learners, and difficult learners.

To teach students with the same method is not suitable for them. If you are a slow learner, this chapter will open your mindset and teach you how to meet up where your teachers' methods fail you. If you follow the steps in this chapter, your IQ will increase, your learning ability will grow, and you'd have become a fast learner before you know it. But first, you must believe that you are intelligent. You must change the way you see yourself.

Let's start with this affirmation and repeat, *"No matter how people see me, no matter my last position in the class. I am intelligent. I am a genius. I am not dull. God created me; therefore, I am intelligent. I will find new ways to learn. I am on my way to success."*

Our environment has the power to affect how we see things and behave. For instance, when someone travels to Europe, Canada, or the United States of America to study and return a few years later, you will notice a significant amount of positive change in the way he/she sees things. However, it depends on that someone because we all assimilate information differently. What is the secret? These countries are ahead of us; they have more efficient school systems and teaching methods. Their teachers and professors are better trained and certified professionals. When they meet their students for the first time, they figure out the students' needs, strengths, and weaknesses, to determine the best ways to teach them. Many of them are more patient—their government's fund States' school systems. Here in Nigeria, the reverse is the case. Most teachers do not know their students, do not make efforts to know them or understand them or what they may be going through.

For instance, many slow and difficult learners are shy students. They hardly ask or answer questions in class. When they do not understand the subject matter, they pretend to know because they are timid to raise hands in class. These types of students suffer silently due to our teaching methods.

The only difference between a fast learner and the rest is that fast learners learn quickly while others do not. However, teachers favor fast learners more than others. Teachers are more kind and friendly to fast learners, ignoring difficult and slow learners. As far as the fast learners understand their lectures, their job is done.

Now, how do you solve this problem? Would you change our school system? I know you wish you can, but the truth is you cannot. Would you change your teachers? That is not possible. But you can change yourself. You can change the way you study. If you are a problematic learner, then you need to be taught many times before you understand. Knowing your teachers are not patient with you, teach yourself. If you are a slow or difficult learner, read more, study more, and focus more. That is the secret. Start teaching yourself. Do not learn. Be patient to understand. Understand the topic in question before focusing on the next topic. Do not be in a hurry. You are not competing with anybody. You are learning according to your God-given capacity to learn. Read until you understand what you are reading. If it takes a fast learner a one-time reading to understand and takes you triple the time to read and understand the same topic, do not worry. Remain focused. In doing so, you are developing your memory to be patient to understand. Intelligence has a lot to do with remembering and applying what you are taught or learning. Self-study allows you to expand your ability to remember, which in turn, increases your intelligence quotient.

Studying is like a child learning how to walk. He stands and falls, stands again, and falls. He takes a few steps, maybe one or two, and falls again. Though he falls, he is slowly developing his muscles and bones. If he continues at it, his bones and muscles will become strong and firm one day, and he would start to walk steadily. A child may learn and walk well in a month; another child may take six months to do the same. Eventually, the two children will walk without support. This is also true of academic learning.

If a problematic learner is determined and continues to be patient, he will develop his brain muscles and the ability to remember and equally reach where the fast learner is.

Another essential mental exercise is to learn a new English word every day or every other day. Any term or sentence that sounds foreign to you look it up in the dictionary. Know the meaning, how to use it, and then start using it appropriately. Remember, if you do not use and speak the new vocabulary, you will forget it…naturally. In doing so, you are developing your mental capacity and growing your IQ.

If you want to be a bodybuilder, you must exercise regularly to tone your muscles. If you do not exercise regularly, your muscles become flat and weak. That is also true about learning. If you do not give your brain little assignments to remember, your mind will become weakened. Many call *'dull brain.'* No brain is dull. The brain is simply not put to good use. Therefore, always put your brain to good use, even if it means starting from learning English alphabets all over again. Just bear in mind that you are teaching your brain how to study and remember. That is what intelligence is all about: study and memorize.

If being a difficult learner means the end of education, Dr. Usman Khadiri would not have become a medical doctor. He told me that he used to be one of the most unintelligent students in his Junior Secondary School class. But today, he runs a very successful private hospital in Kano, Nigeria. The secret of success was his decision to study harder and become one of the best students in his class, if not the best. He was determined to become better and successful, and he became better and successful. I asked him to explain how students should apply these principles, and he said he began a journey of self-education and started to teach himself. There is no student more determined than the one who resolved to learn.

My own school life was almost the same as Dr. Khadiri. When I set the goal to pursue a law degree, I began a self-study journey in the subjects – English Language, English Literature, Government, Economics, History. When I realized that the English Language was an essential subject, I saved money and bought expired and old newspapers. I was reading the newspapers and increasing my vocabulary. When I came across a new word or grammar that enticed me, I quickly looked up the meaning. I started looking for an opportunity to speak about it and brag about it to my friends. I can still remember the first time I came across the word 'junta' in NewsWatch Magazine. Human Rights attorney Gani Fawehinmi was interviewed, and he called Babangida's Government a *'junta.'* The word instantly appealed to me, and I searched for its meaning.

You don't need to buy old newspapers to learn new vocabulary. The bottom line is to form the habit of learning from any suitable source. Open your mind and senses to knowledge. What you learn becomes your personal intellectual property.

Brian Tracy is a successful coach and a leader on human potential. He is a very successful man. His success story started when he was still a young boy. As a teenager, Brian and his two friends decided to travel from America to Africa by road. It sounds crazy for sure, but they were determined. It was very risky. At every point on their road trip, there was an obstacle. Finally, when they got to the Sahara Desert, they became stranded. With the temperature as high as 120 degrees Fahrenheit and thousands of miles still ahead, there seemed to be no hope. They finally passed Lagos, Nigeria, and arrived in Cape Town, South Africa.

That experience changed Brain's life forever. It made him realize early in life that there is nothing you want to be or do and put your heart into, that you cannot be and do. It was why he said, "It doesn't matter who you are, sooner or later, everyone has a Sahara to cross." He wrote a book about his longest journey and titled it, *'Success is a Journey.'* Get you a copy of it, and learn from his experience.

Brian Tracy wrote, *"You have within you right now; everything you need to deal with whatever the world can throw at you."*
If you consider education and success important to you, you have everything within you right now. I am not the one who said it. Even Brian Tracy was merely repeating what many philosophers have long said. You have everything within you right now to become a good student and a successful person. So, stop giving excuses.

YOUR CAREER PATH

There is a significant advantage when you choose a career early in life. When students decide what they want to be, they focus and be determined to study in that direction. They would make more effort more than other students who are yet to decide.

When you decide your career path early, your love for your intended career choice becomes your motivation. So, do not be afraid to choose a career to allow you to be on your chosen field path. If you do not choose a career, you may end up becoming *"Jack of all trades and master of none,"* studying all the subjects, but you will not be master any. Choosing a career early is like going hunting. A good hunter aims at the prey before he shoots. If he aims to shoot at the sky and misses, his bullet may hit the moon. Hitting the moon is also a good shot. It is better than a hunter who shoots without aiming. Such a hunter would be wasting his bullets. If you aim early to study Medicine, naturally, your subject's focus would be on Biology, Health Science, Physics, Chemistry, Mathematics, and English. You would pay more attention to them than you would pay a subject like Economics. When you focus on those needed subjects and master them, you will most likely become a Medical Doctor. But if you miss your target as a doctor, you could become a Pharmacist or any other related medical field.

When I reflect on my life, it was when I chose Law as my career choice that I started to take subjects like Government, English Language, and Literature, Economics, and History seriously.

HOW DO I CHOSE A CAREER?

Did you know that many professionals do not like their jobs? Many of them are unhappy and unfulfilled about the industry they are in. They may be earning high income but miserable and feel stuck. Money is a necessity but does not buy peace of mind. The question becomes, WHY? Well, because the jobs they do for a living are not related to their life purposes. God gave each of us an assignment to do. When God gives you an assignment, He also gives you the spiritual, mental, and physical abilities to fulfill it.

God is the Inventor. He is the Creator. When your work is not related to the passion God put inside you, then you will never be fulfilled. Whenever the hunter dog that hunts cleans his den gun and ready to go hunting, you see the dog happy, running, and wagging its tail. He is about to do the work for which his craftsman crafted him. If you keep that dog, feed it well, send it to any work that is not hunting, the dog will not be happy. That is how humans are too. God gave us different passions. There is a reason you are the Mathematician in your family. The reason you are not a nurse because you hate the sight of blood, or hate injustice and like arguing because you want to be a lawyer, or simply love cooking because you love the art of it. These are indicators of the passion God wired in you. Passions are those things you love doing even when no one will pay you for doing them.

You just love doing them. Imagine choosing a career from what you love doing. Imagine earning money from what you love doing. You would have money, cars, a happy family, and then inner joy.

I know many of those reading this book now would say, *"Ah, let me work, have money and cars; I will be happy."* Some of you think money and cars alone bring happiness. That is not true. If it was true, then why have many millionaires committed suicide? If it was true, why did Mr. Lazarus Nwejei jump down from a five-story building and ended his life? He had money, cars, two children, and a beautiful wife.

Certain things lead to fulfillment in a person's life; doing the work you love is one of them; it is the most important. So, in choosing a career, look inward at what you love doing. Parents and guardians make mistakes in choosing careers for their children. Or rather, forcing their choice of careers on them without knowing or wanting to know what they prefer to be in the future. It is selfish of their parents and guardians. They inadvertently killed the dreams of their children and stopped many of them from reaching their destined greatness. You cannot achieve excellence when you are not doing the work you were born to do. Greatness is linked to destiny. Destiny is about doing the work God intends for you to do. So, the shortest road to greatness is to find out God's purpose for your life and pursue it with passion.

This is why Cristiano Ronaldo is a living legend. He is doing what God wired inside him to do. People like Davido, Nkem Owoh, Chimamanda Ngozi Adichie, Kaffy, and thousands of other men and women became great because they followed their passions as God intended for them.

How to be a good student and a successful person

My purpose is to motivate people. I love teaching and encouraging people to become the best that they can ever be. That is the reason I wrote this book. That is also why I founded the New Africa Movement.

But wait! Why am I teaching students to become better and successful? Because this book is not only about how to be a good student, it is also about how to grow into a successful adult. But you cannot be a successful adult when you do not have inner joy at work. You cannot have inner joy when you do not do the work related to your calling.

Do you know how to find a person who is not happy with what he is doing for a living? They are always bitter when they talk about their job, boss, or co-workers. They probably experience insomnia or are depressed.

Remember what I said at the beginning of this book? Please do not repeat my mistakes and those of others. I want you to learn from what we didn't do and should have done. Those whose careers are related to what they love doing do not get lazy, unnecessarily tired, or easily bored. Rather, they have fun while enjoying the money they are making. It's a win-win for them. It can be a win-win for you too.

Jude Ohanele was a very bright and hardworking student. Still, he wasted his time studying Medicine at Ahmadu Bello University, Zaria, Nigeria, before finding out that the core passion God wired inside of him. When he took some medical students on a Medical Exchange Program to Hamburg, Germany, as Student Leader, he realized that his passion was Advocacy and Public Policy Commentary. He quickly abandoned Medicine and pursued his dream.

Today, Jude Ohanele is a Program Director of Development Dynamics. He travels around the world, giving lectures on Women's Rights and Development. He has spoken at many events, including in the United Nations. Bottom-line, Ohanele is a happy and fulfilled man.

Do not wait until you climb to the top of the ladder to discover that the ladder is not secure enough for you to stay on. Choose your career based on your passions, and then you would have succeeded.

Do not follow the footsteps of those unhappy professionals because of the material things they possess. Unfortunately, such lifestyles cannot replace the joy that comes from doing the work God purposed you to do.

Your Mind is Powerful. USE IT!

Do you know that you become whatever you think? *"As a man thinks in his heart, so is he."* If you think of failure all the time, you become a failure. When you think of success all the time, you become a success—all in time. So, let your mind work for you. Always think positive. Always believe that you would become a great person.

Remember I shared with you how the brain functions and that it has the power to attract to you whatever you think about always? Napoleon Hill wrote a powerful book that made him famous. A book I will recommend to any student who sincerely desires to achieve greatness in this life. We live in a toxic world. It has become so toxic that we hate each other just because we feel we have the right to. These days, we hear more sad stories than good stories. Students are not getting enough motivation from our world. Napoleon Hill's book teaches you that you can use your mind to bring about positive results in your life no matter your situation. It is titled *'The Power of Positive Thinking.'* Another helpful book *is 'Tough Times Never Last, But Tough People Do'* by Robert H. Schuller. Read them; make these books your constant companions. Learn from great minds who had lived before us. Learn from their experiences, steps, and ideas that helped them to succeed.

If you desire success, listen to the advice of those who succeeded. Always think big. Think outside the box. Stop thinking of failure as your foundation. Stop thinking that you are not intelligent or worrying about not having a sponsor to further your education. So, start thinking and believing that you are intelligent because you are, and know that at the right time, God will make create the opportunities for you to be the best that He has destined for you to be. Start loving your life.

Once upon a time, a primary school student took the 20th position in a class of 25. His mother was so furious with him and punished him severely. Afterward, she had a conversation with him to encourage him to become better. The moral of the story is that his mom punished him as a form of discipline and instilled confidence and determination in him so much that the boy vowed no longer to bring disgrace to his mother. He started to study harder like he never did before. Guess what? He came first in his class. He was determined, focused, and he succeeded. The boy's name is Waziri Adio, a successful leader and a commentator on public issues. He is currently the Executive Secretary, Nigerian Extractive Industries Transparency Initiative (NEITI). When his mother died, Waziri wrote a touching tribute in her memory, captioned, *"Dreams from My Mother,"* published in THISDAY Newspaper on January 15, 2020. It was a benefitting eulogy to a mother who knew how to teach her son to be a better man.
You, too, can achieve success using the power of positive thinking. What are you waiting for? The time is now! Not tomorrow!

DO NOT WASTE ANOTHER DAY: START NOW

We have come to the end of this book, but it doesn't mean learning stops. You must know that receiving information does not bring success unless you put it into practice. Someone said, *"Knowledge is power, but applied information is more powerful."* Many have so much knowledge yet are lazy to use the information or experience they have gained. True, positive change can be difficult, especially at an older age. It makes us uncomfortable because we are so used to be in our comfort zones.

Abdullahi Musa was twenty-five years old when a bomb exploded in Maiduguri Market and blew off his right hand. With his left arm still intact, Abdullahi started learning how to make use of it. It was a struggle at first, but he eventually mastered it.

Do not be afraid of thinking outside the box or scared; you will fail every day, but it is your chance to learn, become better, grow, and share what we learned. There's no perfect person here on earth. Do not wait for another day to developing ideas or looking into old ideas. Do not wait for school to resume before you start putting the principles into practice. Do not wait for things to get better to be better. The time is now.

Stories allow us to immerse ourselves in someone's past, understand their mindset, learn from their experiences, failures, and success. Stories help us to make sense of the world we live in. Having said these, I will share one more story.

Once upon a time, in a distant country, low-income families could not relate to the rich. Discrimination roamed the fabric of this country. The rich did not care how their ill-treatments affected the poor masses and made it impossible for the poor to become successful. The rich seized their lands and livestock, and their women were forcefully taken away to become concubines. Their laws were written to discriminate against the poor and favor only the rich. Tuition and books were made very unreasonable for the poor to be able to afford it. Therefore, many children from low-income families did not have access to education.

There was a poor older man who went around teaching everyone to be kind to one another. His teachings were different. Many who followed his advice and instructions were happy and came out with good results. So, the poor kept going to him for advice. When the rich heard about this older man, his teachings, and its impact on the poor. They were against his teachings because the man was showing the poor the road to success. A group of the rich plotted against the older man and lied that he was creating a public disturbance in the city. So, one sunny afternoon, they banished him to the forest. But that did not stop the poor from seeking advice from the older man.

There was a boy whose father was amongst the poorest of the poor. He hated the fact that he was born into abject poverty and envied the rich. The boy was always dreaming of a better life and becoming rich. He wanted to be a lawyer, but he knew to become a lawyer could make it easier to escape poverty and become rich. But, the laws of his country made it impossible to study Law.

One day, he decided to visit the older man for advise. He shared his family background and his far-fetched dream to become a lawyer with the old man. When he finished narrating his story, the old man asked the boy to walk with him. They walked on a narrow path that led to a river. When they got to the river, he grabbed the boy by the neck and forced his head into the river, pretending to drown him. The boy was choking on the water while struggling to free himself, but the man held him tight. The boy continued to struggle to break free. He pushed and shoved, but the old man would not let him go. Suddenly, the boy gave the old man a hard push and freed himself.

After the boy was free of the old man's grip, the old man began walking back as nothing had happened. When the boy regained his consciousness, he ran after the man. He caught up with him and quickly grabbed the old man by the waist in deep anger. The old man stopped and said to the boy, *"My son, you said you want to be a lawyer, but your family is poor. When I forced you into the river, you were struggling to free yourself, but you could not. But when it looked like your life was in danger, you used every strength and energy in you to push me away. Now, if you use the same kind of survival instinct and mindset to pursue your dream of becoming a lawyer, or pursue any goal you want in this life, you must surely get it."*

Author's Final Note

I promised at the beginning of this book, and I believe I have kept my promise. If you have read this book up to this point and feel that you did not get anything out of it, please reach out to me; you will get your money back. Better yet, tear the pages to pieces and write to me about it. I will refund your purchase money and apologise for wasting your time. But, If you feel motivated and inspired to thrive in school and become a success, and the impact this book made in your life, please share your experience with me and write a review on Amazon and other online bookstores where this book is sold.

Thank you.

Goddy Obasi

Goddy Obasi is a lawyer, author, motivation philosopher, and Keynote Speaker. He was called to the Nigerian Bar in 2011; he is a graduate of the Imo State University, Owerri, and Institute for African Studies and History. He believes that his mission in life is to motivate young people. He is the founder of the New Africa Movement, a not-for-profit organization that teaches and spreads the campaign of love and tolerance across Africa's divisive tribes and religions. His media broadcast on YouTube channel can be found on Youtube.com/Goddyobasi or www.newafricamovement.org and other social media platforms.